For Christopher
who knows all about being small
—LJ

To all the mommies, big and small
—PM

PUFFIN BOOKS
Published by the Penguin Group
Penguin Putnam Books for Young Readers, 345 Hudson Street, New York, NY 10014, U.S.A.
Penguin Books Ltd, 27 Wrights Lane, London W8 5TZ, England
Penguin Books Canada Ltd, 10 Alcorn Avenue, Toronto, Ontario, Canada M4V 3B2
Penguin Books Ltd, Registered Offices: Harmondsworth, Middlesex, England

First published in the United States of America by G. P. Putnam's Sons,
a division of Penguin Putnam Books for Young Readers, 1997
Published by Puffin Books, a member of Penguin Putnam Books for Young Readers, 1999

1 3 5 7 9 10 8 6 4 2

Text copyright © Lynne Jonell, 1997. Illustrations copyright © Petra Mathers, 1997

THE LIBRARY OF CONGRESS HAS CATALOGED THE PUTNAM EDITION AS FOLLOWS:
Jonell, Lynne. Mommy go away / Lynne Jonell; illustrated by Petra Mathers. p. cm.
Summary: During bathtime, Christopher and his mother share an experience
in which she shrinks to a very small size and he takes care of her.
ISBN 0-399-23001-7
[1. Size–Fiction. 2. Baths–Fiction. 3. Mothers and sons–Fiction.] I. Mathers, Petra, ill. II. Title.
PZ7.J675Mo 1997 [E]–dc20 96-38194 CIP AC

This edition ISBN 0-698-11810-3
Printed in Hong Kong

WRITTEN BY Lynne Jonell

ILLUSTRATED BY Petra Mathers

PUFFIN BOOKS

Mommy said, "Pick up your blocks."

Mommy said, "No more T.V."

Mommy said, "Time for your bath."

Christopher said, "Go away, Mommy!
Go away on this boat!"

Mommy was surprised.
"But this boat is too little."

"You are too big. Be small, Mommy."
So Mommy got small.

"Now stop," said Christopher.
"That's small enough."

"Oh! Oh, my!" said Mommy.
"This is too small for me!
And the boat is so tippy!
And the waves are so big!"

"Good-bye!" called Christopher.
"Have a good time!
Remember your manners!

Don't forget to brush your teeth!
And no hitting the other mommies!"

"Oh, dear," said Mommy.
"There is so much to remember.

What if I forget?"

"I will help you," said Christopher.

"But what if a big sea duck comes
and quacks at me?

And the boat tips over—
and I fall out with
all the other mommies?"

"I will put you on a raft,"
said Christopher.
"But I will get soap in my eyes,"
said Mommy. "And then I will cry."

Christopher laughed.
"You won't cry," he said.
"Mommies are brave."

"Not always," said Mommy.
"Help!"

"Don't worry," said Christopher.
"I will take care of you."
"But I am so little, you might
lose me," Mommy said.

"I will find you," Christopher said.
"And I will dry you off, too."
Mommy looked up.

"I want to be big," she said.
"I want to be big **now**."
"You'll have to ask nicely,"
said Christopher.

"Please?"

"Oh, all right," said Christopher.
"You have been a good mommy.
You can be big again."

"Oh, good," said Mommy.
"It is hard to be so small."

"I know that already,"
said Christopher.